THE
THREE
SILLIES

WALTER
DE LA MARE

CREATIVE EDUCATION INC.

Published by Creative Education, Inc.
123 South Broad Street, Mankato, Minnesota 56001

Designed by Rita Marshall
Cover Illustration by Etienne Delessert

Acknowledgment: The Literary Trustees of Walter de
la Mare and the Society of Authors as their
representative.

Library of Congress Cataloging-in-Publication Data

De la Mare, Walter, 1873–1956.
    The three sillies/by Walter de la Mare.
    p.   cm.
    Summary: A young man believes that his sweetheart
and her family are the silliest people in the world, until
he meets three others who are even sillier.
    ISBN 0-88682-467-2
    [1. Folklore—England.]   I. Title.
PZ8.1.D365Th   1991
398.2—dc20   91-2371
    [E]

To the Continuation

of fine literature for

readers of all ages.

THERE WAS ONCE A FARMER AND HIS WIFE

WHO HAD A DAUGHTER, AND THIS

daughter had a sweetheart, and a gentleman he

was. Three days a week this gentleman used to

come and see the daughter and stay to supper,

and a little before supper time, the daughter

used to go down into the cellar to draw the beer.

■ Now one evening, as the beer was running softly out of the barrel into the jug, she gave a great yawn, and in so doing looked up at the beams of the cellar over her head, and — stuck up there in one of them—she saw an old chopper. It was a broken old rusty chopper, and must have been sticking in the beam there for ages. But as she looked at the chopper—and the beer trickling softly on—she began to think and this is what she thought:

"Now supposing me and my gentleman up there get married soon, and we have a son we do, same as *my* mother and father had a daughter, and that son we have grows up and grows up, and keeps a-growing up, and when at last he's quite grown up he comes down here some evening, same as me here now as you might say, to draw the beer for supper, and that there old chopper comes *whopp* down on his head and chops off his head—My! what a dreadful, dreadful, *dreadful* thing it would be!" At this, she flopped down on the settle beside the cask, and burst out crying.

~~~~~~~~~~~~~~~ Now the farmer and his wife and the gentleman began to want their beer. So the mother went down after her daughter into the cellar, and found her sitting there on the settle beside the barrel, crying and crying, and the beer running out of the jug all over the cellar floor. So she asked her what was the matter.

And the daughter, sobbing and sobbing, said: "Oh Mother, look at that old rusty chopper stuck up in the beam!" Her mother looked at the chopper.

My! WHAT A DREADFUL, DREADFUL, *DREADFUL* THING IT WOULD BE!

"Now just you think, Mother," says she, "supposing now me and my gentlemen up there was to get married soon, and we was to have a son, same as you and father had a daughter,

which was me in a manner of speaking, and that
son was to grow up, and up, and up, and one
day he came stepping down into the cellar to
draw beer, same as we are now, and that old
chopper there stuck in the beam was to come
whopp down and chop his head off, what a
dreadful, dreadful, *dreadful* thing it would be!"

At this the farmer's wife, looking at the chopper, could contain herself no longer, but
flopped down on the settle beside her daughter
and burst out crying. So there sat the two of

them. By-and-by the gentleman says to the farmer, "What about that beer?" So down came the farmer after his wife and his daughter and the beer; and there was the beer running all over the cellar floor.

■ "Why, whatever is the matter?" said the farmer.

The old wife told him just what the daughter had said. And when the farmer looked at the rusty chopper stuck in the beam, he could contain himself no more, and "Oh," said he, "what a dreadful, dreadful, *dreadful* thing it would

be!" And down he squatted beside the other

two on the settle, and burst out a-crying.

So at last the gentleman upstairs, being as dry

Aｎᴅ ᴅᴏᴡɴ ʜᴇ sǫᴜᴀᴛᴛᴇᴅ ʙᴇsɪᴅᴇ

ᴛʜᴇ ᴏᴛʜᴇʀ ᴛᴡᴏ ᴏɴ ᴛʜᴇ sᴇᴛᴛʟᴇ, ᴀɴᴅ

ʙᴜʀsᴛ ᴏᴜᴛ ᴀ-ᴄʀʏɪɴɢ.

as an oven, came down into the cellar to look

for the farmer and the farmer's wife and their

daughter and the beer; and there were these

boobies, all three of them, sitting side by side

on the settle, and crying and crying; and there was the beer trickling down all over the floor, and more of it out of the cask, by a long chalk, than in it. So the gentleman first turned off the tap, then asked them what they were all sitting there crying for.

And "Oh," said they together, "look at that horrid old rusty chopper stuck in the beam. Supposing you were to have a son, and he grew up, and up, and up, and one evening, same as might be now, he came down here to draw beer and it fell down *whopp* on his head and chopped his head off, what a dreadful, dread-

ful, *dreadful* thing it would be!"

■ At this the gentleman burst out laughing.

"Well," says he, "of all the sillies I ever set eyes

on, you three are the silliest. That's just done

for me! Off I go to-morrow morning, but I

promise you this—if ever I find three sillies sil-

lier than you three sillies, I'll come back there

and then, and we'll have the wedding." So off

he went.

~~~~~~~~~~ Day after day the

gentleman ambled along on his fat, red-roan

mare, enjoying his travels, and at last he came

to a cottage. It was an old cottage, and wallflow-

ers were blowing in the garden, and very sweet

too; and up there on the roof under its chimney

"WELL," SAYS HE, "OF ALL THE

SILLIES I EVER SET EYES ON, YOU

THREE ARE THE SILLIEST."

were not only snapdragons and cat's valerian,

but tufts of grass sprouting out of the thatch;

and leaning against the thatch was a ladder. It

was at *this* the gentleman stared for the old

woman of the cottage was doing her utmost to push her old cow up this ladder, but the cow wouldn't.

THE GENTLEMAN AMBLED ALONG

ON HIS FAT, RED-ROAN MARE,

ENJOYING HIS TRAVELS

"Kem over!" she says. "Upadaisy!" she says; and there was the cow shooing and mooing and not daring to go.

The gentleman looking down from his horse said, "What's going on, dame?" The old woman told the gentleman that she was trying to get her cow up on to the roof so that she could eat the juicy tufts of fresh, green, beautiful grass up there under the chimney.

"Then when I have got her on to the roof," she said, "I shall tie the end of this here rope round her neck, and drop the other end down the chimney, and tie *that* end round my arm. So that way," she says, "I shall know if my old cow's safe on the roof or not."

"Well, well, well!" said the gentleman, and went on watching her. After a long time the old woman managed to do what she wanted, and there sat her cow on the thatch—all legs, horns, and tail—and a strange sight *she* was. But the moment the old woman had gone into the house, the poor old cow slipped on the thatch, and down she came, dangling by the rope round her neck, and was strangled. As for the old woman tied up to the rope by her arm inside the house, when the cow came down, up went she, and was jammed up inside the chimney and smothered in the soot.

Then of course the neighbours came running out; and the gentleman rode off on his horse; and as he went he thought to himself: "Well, of all the silly sillies that was *one!*"

■ He travelled on and on, and came one night to an inn. This inn happening to be full of company, there was only one way, the landlord told the gentleman, for him to sleep, and that was with a stranger in a great, double bed. So, as there was nothing better, he hung up his hat, went downstairs for some supper, came back, and after a bit of talking together he and the stranger were soon fast asleep in the great four-post bed.

As he went he thought to himself: "WELL, OF ALL THE SILLY SILLIES THAT WAS *ONE!*"

When, about seven, the gentleman awoke in the morning, what should he see but that this stranger had hung up his breeches on to the two top knobs of the chest-of-drawers; and there he was, running to and fro, up the room and down again, trying might and main to *jump* into his breeches. First he got one leg in—that was no good. The next time he got the other leg in—that was no better. Sometimes neither leg went in, and that was worse. And he never got both. At last he stopped to take breath, and, mopping his head, said to the gentleman in the bed:

"My! You wouldn't believe it, but it takes me the best part of a solid hour every morning to get into those breeches of mine. How do you manage with yours?"

"Well, well, well!" said the gentleman, bursting out laughing. And he showed him.

As after breakfast he was mounting his horse —which the ostler had brought out of the sta-

---

"WELL, WELL, WELL!" SAID THE GENTLEMAN, BURSTING OUT LAUGHING.

---

ble—the gentleman suddenly thought of his bed-fellow and the breeches again, and burst out laughing. "Well, of silly sillies," he said to himself, "hang me if that wasn't a sillier silly still."

Off he went on his travels again, and at last came to a pretty village down Somerset way, with fine green trees in it and a pond. But quiet village it certainly was not, for all about this

"WELL, OF SILLY SILLIES," HE SAID TO HIMSELF, "HANG ME IF THAT WASN'T A SILLIER SILLY STILL."

pond seemed to be collected the people for miles around, some with hayrakes, and some with brooms and besoms, and some with pitch-forks; and there they were, all of them, raking and scrabbling, and scrabbling and raking in the water.

"Why," said the gentleman, "what's the matter?"

"Matter!" said they "well, you may ask it. Last night the old green moon tumbled into the pond, for old Gaffer Giles, coming home, looked in and saw her there, and we can't fetch her out nohow."

"Moon!" said the gentleman, bursting out laughing. "Wait till evening, my friends, and if she don't come swimming up into the East

there, as right as ninepence, I'll eat my hat!"

But this only made them angry, and with their

Taking thirty or forty heads
for one; they were the very
worst silly I've ever seen."

---

brooms and pitchforks and hayrakes they

chased the gentlemen and his horse out of the

village.

"Well," said the gentleman to himself, as he

rode off down the hill, *"well,* taking thirty or

forty heads for one; they were the very worst

silly I've ever seen."

■ So, true to his word, he turned back again,

and a week or two after reached the farm and

married the farmer's daughter. And that being

so, maybe he was the silliest silly of *all* silly

sillies. But who's to say?

~~~~~~~~~~~~~